CHARLIE & MOUSE
OUTDOORS

By **LAUREL SNYDER**   Illustrated by **EMILY HUGHES**

chronicle books · san francisco

For Mose and Lewis (and Uncle Roy),
who know about the zoomies —L. S.

To Jerson —E. H.

Library of Congress Cataloging-in-Publication Data:

Names: Snyder, Laurel, author. | Hughes, Emily (Illustrator), illustrator.
Title: Charlie & Mouse outdoors / by Laurel Snyder ; illustrated by Emily Hughes.
Other titles: Charlie and Mouse outdoors
Description: San Francisco : Chronicle Books, [2019] | Summary: Charlie and
Mouse and their parents are going on a camping trip, and there will be
hiking, storytelling, marshmallows, and campfires, and the joy that comes
from sharing it all.
Identifiers: LCCN 2017045866 | ISBN 9781452170664 (alk. paper)
Subjects: LCSH: Brothers—Juvenile fiction. | Camping—Juvenile fiction. |
Families—Juvenile fiction. | CYAC: Brothers—Fiction. | Camping—Fiction.
| Family life—Fiction.
Classification: LCC PZ7.S6851764 Cn 2019 | DDC [E]—
dc23 LC record available at https://lccn.loc.gov/2017045866

Manufactured in China.

Design by Jennifer Tolo Pierce.
Typeset in Baskerville.
The illustrations in this book were rendered
by hand in graphite and with Photoshop.

10 9 8 7 6 5 4 3 2 1

Chronicle Books LLC
680 Second Street
San Francisco, California 94107

Chronicle Books—we see things differently.
Become part of our community at www.chroniclekids.com.

Contents

BORING

Charlie was in the car.

Mouse was in the car.

Charlie and Mouse were in the car.

"This is boring," said Charlie.

"Why don't you make up a story," said Dad.

"Stories aren't boring."

"I will try," said Charlie.

The car went over a great green mountain.

"Once upon a time," said Charlie, "there was

a great green mountain."

"Then what happened?" asked Mouse.

"I do not know," said Charlie. "I will think

about it."

The car went past a small white house.

"Once upon a time," said Charlie, "there

was a small white house near a great green

mountain."

"Then what happened?" asked Mouse.

Charlie sighed. "I do not know. It is hard to

make up a story."

The car went past a field.

There was a hawk over the field.

The hawk had something *wiggling* in its mouth.

"Once upon a time," said Charlie, "there was a

hawk, and something was *wiggling* in its mouth."

"Ooh!" said Mouse. "Then what happened?"

"The wiggling thing turned out to be a . . .

dragon!" said Charlie.

"Wow! *Then* what happened?" asked Mouse.

"The dragon and the hawk had a battle in the

sky! The dragon spit fire, and they both flapped

their wings so hard that it rained!"

Suddenly, it began to rain.

"Oh my!" said Mom.

"Quick, Charlie!" said Mouse. "Tell us a

different story."

"Once upon a time," said Charlie. "Dad stopped the car. And we had french fries until the rain stopped."

"I like this story," said Mouse.

THE HIKE

A hike! A hike!

It was time for a hike!

Charlie and Mouse walked along the stream.

Mom and Dad walked, too.

There was a trail.

The trail was pine needles and bits of sun.

Charlie found a stick.

Mouse found a stick.

They were very good sticks.

"NOW," said Charlie. "This is our land and

we must defend it from bad guys!"

Charlie and Mouse defended the land.

"NOW," said Mouse. "We are in monster

country, and the monsters are coming!"

"Monsters, begone!" shouted Charlie.

Charlie and Mouse fought the monsters.

"Oh no, look!" said Mouse, pointing into a bush.

"Good eye, Mouse," said Charlie. "We must

be careful! Danger is all around us."

"What is it now?" asked Mom.

"A lion," said Mouse. "A hungry one."

"Oh no," said Dad. "Will you save us?"

"Save yourselves!" shouted Charlie. He ran

at the bush. "AAAGH!"

"Whew!" said Mouse, when the battle was over.

"That was a close one."

"My strength is fading," said Charlie.

"Mine, too," said Mouse. He sat on a rock.

"Would a granola bar help?" asked Dad.

"It might," said Mouse.

Mouse ate a granola bar.

Charlie ate a granola bar.

"Look," said Charlie, "I see a turtle."

"Yes," said Mom.

"Look," said Mouse, "I see a mushroom."

"Look," said Charlie. "I see a—"

"PIG!" shouted Mouse. He jumped up.

"PIG!" shouted Charlie.

The pig snorfled off.

"There are pigs here?" asked Mouse.

"You did not say there would be pigs!"

Charlie and Mouse ran back to the tent.

They zipped it up tight.

KITTENS

"I did not like that pig," said Mouse.

"No," said Charlie. "I did not like it either."

"What else do you think is *out there*?" Mouse asked.

"Other scary stuff?"

"Try not to think about it," said Charlie.

"I cannot help it," said Mouse.

"Yes, you can," said Charlie. "You just need

to think of something else."

"Like what?" asked Mouse.

"Something not scary," said Charlie.

"Like swinging on a swing!"

"Sometimes, swinging is scary to me,"

said Mouse.

"Oh," said Charlie. "Well, how about swimming?"

"Swimming is *always* a little bit scary,"

said Mouse.

"You know what isn't ever scary?"

asked Charlie. "Kittens!"

"That's true," said Mouse. "Kittens are little

and fuzzy. They are not scary at all."

"Let's think of kittens," said Charlie.

"Okay," said Mouse.

"Oh! I see a kitten!" said Mouse. "He is orange!

And nice. He *is* nice."

"My kitten is gray," said Charlie. "My kitten

is named Smoke."

"My kitten is named Ginger," said Mouse.

"Ginger and Smoke!" said Charlie.

"Ginger and Smoke!" said Mouse.

"Look," said Charlie. "Smoke is chasing his tail!

Silly Smoke."

"Look!" said Mouse. "Now, Ginger has the

zoomies! He is zooming."

"Smoke has the zoomies, too!" said Charlie.

"He's zooming on *me*!"

"Now Smoke is jumping on Ginger!" said Mouse.

"Watch out, Ginger. I'll save you!"

Then—CRASH went the tent.

"That," said Charlie, "was a little bit scary."

"Yes," said Mouse. "It was. But it was also

a lot of fun."

THE FIRE

It was getting dark.

"Is it time?" asked Charlie.

"Yes," said Dad. "It's time."

Charlie and Mouse sat on big rocks near

the fire.

Mouse brought Blanket.

"Blanket has never seen a fire," said Mouse.

Mom lit the match.

Charlie and Mouse watched.

First the little sticks caught fire.

Then the big sticks caught fire.

The sky got darker.

Dad handed out marshmallows.

Mouse ate his.

Charlie put his marshmallow on a stick.

He held it in the fire.

"Do not hold it so close to the fire," Dad said.

"It will burn."

"I know what to do!" said Charlie.

Charlie's marshmallow burst into flame.

Charlie blew on it. The flame went away.

The marshmallow was black and crinkly.

"Do you need a new marshmallow?" asked Dad.

Charlie shook his head. "No, I like them like this."

"You do?" said Mouse.

Charlie ate the black marshmallow.

It turned out . . . he DID like them like that.

Then . . .

The fire crackled.

Bugs chirped.

An owl made a HOOOOOOOO sound.

Mouse leaned against Mom.

Charlie leaned against Dad.

After a while Charlie said, "Does anyone

want to tell a story?"

Nobody answered.

Charlie looked around.

Charlie smiled.

Charlie whispered,

"Once upon a time . . .

everyone was very, very happy."